How to WALK an ANT

BY Cindy DERBY

Roaring Brook Press New York

My name is Amariyah,
and I am an Expert Walker.

No, I don't mean I walk perfect,
I mean I walk things.

NOT dogs.

NOT fancy little gnomes.

And NOT goldfish.

My specialty is . . .

STEP ONE

ANT?

Find Ant

Ants can be found in or on trees,
water fountains, or even better . . .
abandoned candy canes.

Tip

Look for ant scouts.
They are more open to possibility.

Rule

Look left then right when
crossing ant highways.

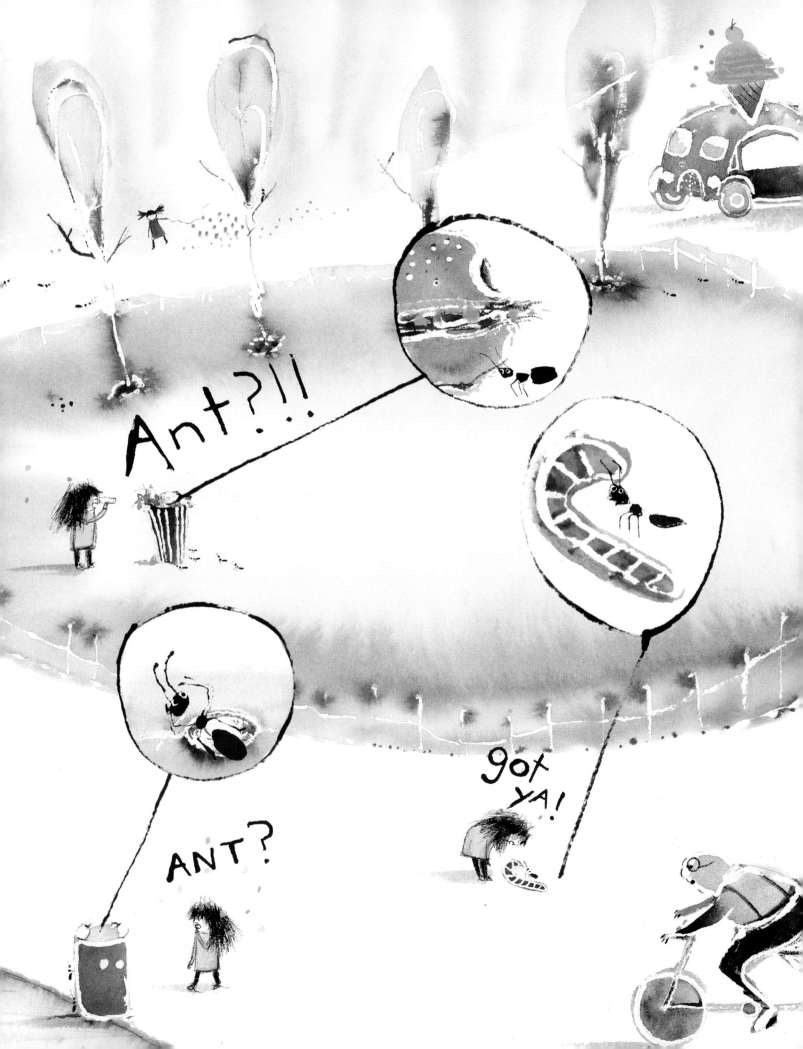

Step Two

Politely Introduce Yourself

Tip

Remain calm.

Rule

Don't be antsy.
Ants can smell fear with their ANTennae.

Step Three

Gain Their Trust

Tip

Use a bridge. Sticks, leaves, or your grandmother's fake nail.*

ooo... la la......

Rule

Don't stab the ant.**

Tip

Prove to them how loyal you are.

BFF

we aRe SUCH AMAzing fRiends, I got A tattoo of you ON MY ARM!

Rule

Use semipermanent ink, as relationships may alter with time.

*Fake nails can be found under the sofa.
**Please refer to "How to Conduct a Funeral" in appendix 1.

STEP FOUR

Prepare the Leash

Tie the smallest bow in the universe then secure the leash between the ant's thorax and head.***

Tip
Like this

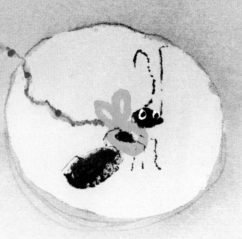

Rule
Not this

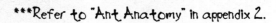

***Refer to "Ant Anatomy" in appendix 2.

STeP FiVe

Make a Goal

Tip

Walking to the ice cream truck is an excellent goal.
The Estimated Ant Travel Time (EATT) without
traffic is 35.7 minutes.

Rule

Stay on designated path.
There may be dangers.

STEP SIX
Control the Leash

TIP

If your ant takes a wrong turn,
shorten the leash 4 centimeters.

Ok then...

Really?!

WOW.

A Retired
Clowns

Guide
to Life

STEP SEVEN
Practice How to Walk

Tip

Reward the ant with one lick of candy cane every 7 centimeters.

Rule

Watch your back . . .

When you encounter a colony of ants repeat steps two through seven three thousand and twenty-eight times.

STEP EIGHT

Tip

And whatever you do...

don't...get...

Step Nine

Celebrate when you reach your goal.

APPeNDiX 1

How to Conduct a Funeral

Tip Popsicle sticks make great tombstones!

APPeNDix 2

Ant Anatomy

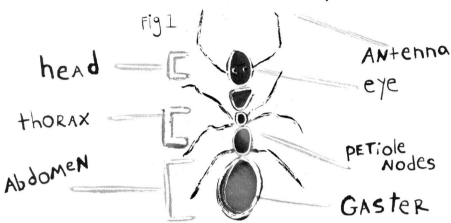

Fig 1

head

thorax

Abdomen

ANtenna

eye

PETiole Nodes

GASTeR

GLOSSARY

Ant Highway: When ants find an abandoned ice cream cone or candy cane, they march together in a line to collect the food and bring it back to their colony. They know where to go because they leave behind a pheromone.

POOF!

Pheromone: A weird smelling chemical that ants produce so that they know their way around. Think of it like stinky fart that only ants can smell.

bye, sweetheart! you don't ever have to COME HOME!

Ant Scout: Brave ants that wander off from the rest of the colony to find food. These ants are the best to walk because they don't have a curfew.

Antville POPULATION 5,000,000,000,000

Ant Colony: Ants are social insects and live in gigantic organized structures called colonies. Some colonies are so big, they house millions of ants. That's why it's important to carry around extra thread.

SNiFF SNiFF

Antennae: These are what ants use to smell pheromones left by other ants. When two ants meet, they sniff each other.

The ANT and LADYBUG WALKING EXPERTS
Next ANT and LADYBUG WALKING TOUR begins Tomorrow
DISPLAY ONLY

For Ms. Moretti, who believes in students with outlandish ideas. —C.D.

Copyright © 2019 by Cindy Derby

Published by Roaring Brook Press

Roaring Brook Press is a division of Holtzbrinck Publishing Holdings Limited Partnership

175 Fifth Avenue, New York, NY 10010

mackids.com

Library of Congress Control Number: 2018944874

ISBN: 978-1-250-16262-5

Our books may be purchased in bulk for promotional, educational, or business use. Please contact
your local bookseller or the Macmillan Corporate and Premium Sales Department at (800) 221-7945 ext. 5442
or by e-mail at MacmillanSpecialMarkets@macmillan.com.

First edition, 2019

Printed in China by RR Donnelley Asia Printing Solutions Ltd., Dongguan City, Guangdong Province

1   3   5   7   9   10   8   6   4   2